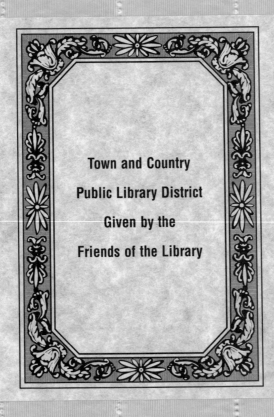

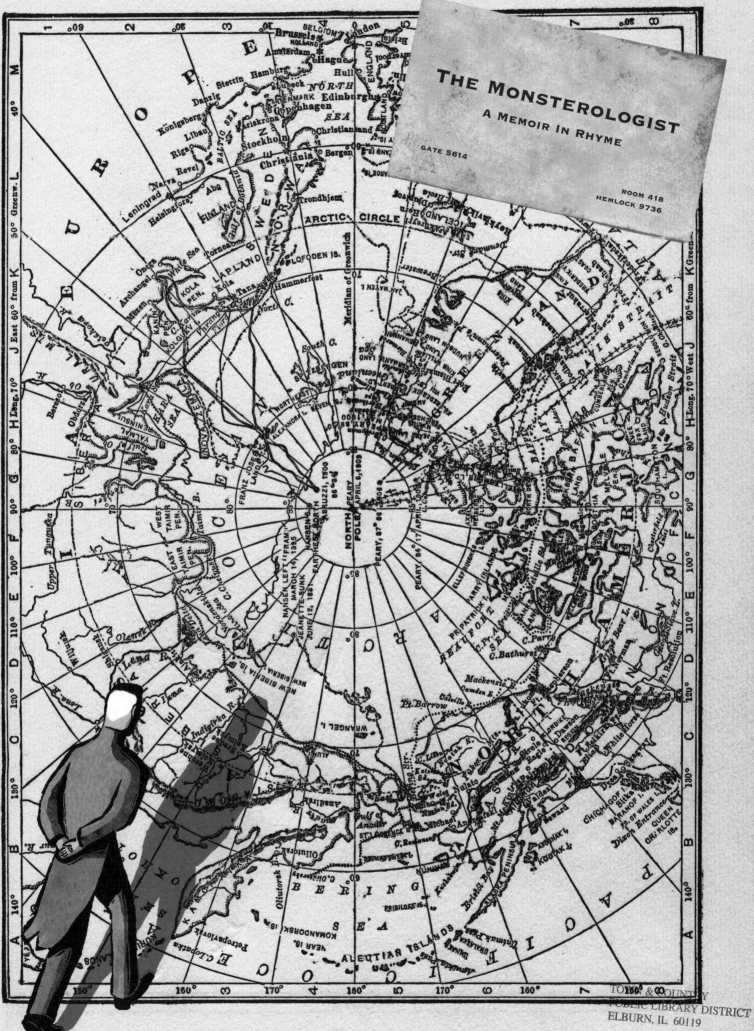

THE MONSTEROLOGIST
A MEMOIR IN RHYME

GATE 5614

ROOM 418
HEMLOCK 9736

For Antonio, William, and my two bewitching friends, Ujjala and Karen. –B.K.

For Spazzo Nandi Duke Kahanamoku and, with a great tip of the hat, Thos. E. Hill. –A.M.

A Preliminary Note

An only child, a lonely child—
my pair of parents rarely smiled—
I turned to books for company.
The paranormal hummed to me!
By age ten, I'd mastered Greek
(one of thirteen tongues I speak).
Attending universities,
I earned a gaggle of degrees
(in sciences, philosophies...)
What I learned, O reader dear,
launched me on my grand career.

— *The Monsterologist*

The illustrations for this book were created using: lots of paper, spaghetti, twigs, tape, paint, file folders, rubber stamps, a scanner, old sketchbooks, new sketchbooks, a printer, a ballpoint pen, a Xerox machine, scraperboard, computer programs, clip art, things found on the street, and some string. Oh yeah, and a few brains and hands.

STERLING and the distinctive Sterling logo are registered trademarks of Sterling Publishing Co., Inc.

Library of Congress Cataloging-in-Publication Data

Katz, Bobbi.
    The monsterologist : a memoir in rhyme / by Bobbi Katz ; illustrated by Adam McCauley.
        p. cm.
    ISBN 978-1-4027-4417-4
    1. Monsters--Juvenile poetry. 2. Ghosts--Juvenile poetry.
    3. Children's poetry, American. I. McCauley, Adam, ill. II. Title.

    PS3561.A7518M58 2009
    811'.54--dc22

                                                2008042794

10 9 8 7 6 5 4 3 2 1

Published by Sterling Publishing Co., Inc.
387 Park Avenue South, New York, NY 10016
Distributed in Canada by Sterling Publishing
c/o Canadian Manda Group, 165 Dufferin Street
Toronto, Ontario, Canada M6K 3H6
Distributed in the United Kingdom by GMC Distribution Services
Castle Place, 166 High Street, Lewes, East Sussex, England BN7 1XU
Distributed in Australia by Capricorn Link (Australia) Pty. Ltd.
P.O. Box 704, Windsor, NSW 2756, Australia

Printed in Thailand in April 2009
All rights reserved

Sterling ISBN 978-1-4027-4417-4

For information about custom editions, special sales, premium and corporate purchases, please contact Sterling Special Sales Department at 800-805-5489 or specialsales@sterlingpublishing.com.

DESIGNED BY CYNTHIA WIGGINTON

CT. VL. DRACULA
BRAN, TRANSYLVANIA
507025

ROMANIA
15 B

The Monsterologist
A MEMOIR IN RHYME

ghostwritten by Bobbi Katz
illustrated by Adam McCauley

STERLING
New York / London
www.sterlingpublishing.com/kids

Contents

MEET A MONSTEROLOGIST...8

FROM THE DESK OF COUNT DRACULA...10

TROLLS.............11

THE TRUTH ABOUT THE OGRE..........12

WEREWOLF WARNING........13

UNDERSTANDING GRENDEL........14

THE GOLEM........18

MEDUSA..................20

CYCLOPS..............21

GHOST NOTES......................22

MY FAVORITE THINGS......24

PING-PONG WITH KING KONG...26

CHILLING GODZILLA.........................27

BLUEBEARD'S PERSONAL AD...28

ADVICE FROM FRANKENSTEIN'S MONSTER...29

AN INTERVIEW WITH THE LOCH NESS MONSTER...32

THE KRAKEN.........................35

THE YETI.........................36

THE COMPU-MONSTER.........................37

THE VERBIVORE.........................38

THE SUDS-SURFING SOCK-EATER...40

INTERNATIONAL ZOMBIE SURVEY...42

A SUGGESTION FOR MY READERS...46

Meet a Monsterologist

To learn about birds,
consult an ornithologist.
To learn just what makes people tick,
seek out a wise psychologist.
But...
if monsters are what interest you,
the how and why of what they do,
I know the facts: What's false, what's true,
since I'm a monsterologist.

I've traveled all around the world
to study and observe.
At times I have been terrified
but I've *never* lost my nerve.

The choicest fruits of my research
are in this rare collection
of letters, notes, and interviews
compiled for your inspection.

My Dear Friend,

    I'm the Count whom you can count on for hospitality.
When you visit Transylvania, be sure to stay with me.
My ancient castle's gloomy, but you'll have a lovely room
conveniently located…close to the family tomb.

    Just buy a one-way ticket. There's no need to splurge.
I'd really love to see you. It's an overwhelming urge.
You'll find that I'm a genial host,
    but at times I think I'll burst,
    unless I drink a bit of blood to satisfy my thirst.
    A friendly nip, a little sip is harmless, you'll agree.
It's natural and organic, and my castle is smoke-free.

    Please hurry, hurry, hurry! No need to R.S.V.P.
I can hardly wait to see you. Please come and visit me.

    Yours, truly, most cordially,

                          The Count

BRAN, TRANSYLVANIA 507025

TROLLS

In days of yore the ghastly trolls
patrolled the roads, demanding tolls.
The fate of those who could not pay
is just too horrible to say.
The trolls, who never brushed their teeth,
had pointy chins with beards beneath
all full of moss and dried-up crud
like soft-boiled eggs and sausage blood.

Nowadays we don't hear much
of ghastly trolls with beards and such.
Yet we're still stopped and we pay tolls
but just to ordinary souls.

Or **are** they "ordinary souls"?
Could it be that **some** are...trolls?

The Truth about the Ogre

IT'S TRUE THAT THE OGRE IS GRUMPY
AND LIVES BY HIMSELF IN A CAVE,
PICKING HIS NOSE WITH A FISH HOOK—
REFUSING TO SHOWER OR SHAVE.
BUT
    THE
        OGRE
            DOES
                not
                    FEAST
                        ON
                            humans!
(THEY'RE TOO HIGH IN CHOLESTEROL.)
HE EATS ROTTEN FRUIT AND RAW VEGGIES
THAT HE STORES IN A CRACKED TOILET BOWL.

WEREWOLF WARNING

If the palm
of the hand
you're shaking
is sprouting hair,
BEWARE!
It means you've just met a werewolf,
or maybe you've met a werebear.
The creature might be very charming,
suggesting a date to meet soon.
Smile politely,
agree...
then *skedaddle.*
Don't wait for the next full moon!

13

UNDERSTANDING GRENDEL

DANISH PASTRY

TAKE HALF A DOZEN DOZING DANES.

SPLIT THEIR SKULLS.

PULL OUT THEIR BRAINS.

TEAR OFF ARMS.

TEAR OFF LEGS.

ADD FLOUR TO

WELL-BEATEN EGGS

FOLD IN DANES

AND YOU WILL GET

A PASTRY TO EAT

BAKED OR WET.

Mother's Recipe

OPTIONAL:

GARNISH WITH A LIMB OR TWO

OR SAVE TO USE

IN SOUP OR STEW.

Many centuries ago, long before my birth,
the monster Grendel roared a roar,
     then stomped
          across
               the earth.
All I knew about him were stories that I read:
Beowulf killed Grendel. For years they've both been dead.
Grendel is still famous for his dreadful appetite:
sneaking snacks of snoozing Danes, noshing every night.

Grendel had a mom, they say, who doted on her son.
She called him "Tootsie-Wootsie" and "Mommy's Honey Bun."
Yet I suspect that Grendel was tutored by none other
to indulge his crude food cravings by his very monstrous...
     mother!
I happened upon evidence that makes me think this way,
when wandering in Denmark on a hiking holiday.
Exploring a dank mossy cave, what did I see?
A moldy piece of parchment with this ancient recipe:

THE GOLEM

The Golem was made by a wizard,
a most learned rabbi, they say.
Its main job was beating up bullies,
although it was just made of clay.

The Golem could leap from the rooftops
or dive to the depths of the sea,
collecting a net full of fishes
which the wizard then passed out for free.

The Golem got its magic power
from a paper stuck into its ear.
The wizard wrote secrets upon it
that only the Golem could hear.

The Golem could work like a robot
or fly like a plane on the breeze.
(And the Golem would probably do homework,
if kids were polite and said "please.")

The Golem was such a kind monster.
Too bad it's no longer about.
Perhaps its ear itched and it scratched it,
and the magical paper fell out.

In ancient Greece they made a fuss
about their hero Perseus.
They sang of monsters that he slew,
but I believe he missed these two.

ATHENS

Medusa

JUST ONE LOOK AT MEDUSA

COULD TURN YOU TO STONE.

WHEN SHE SAYS, "LET'S TALK,"

PLAY IT SAFE. USE THE PHONE.

SHE'S A VERY VAIN MONSTER,

BUT SHE'LL *never* SAY,

"I'M HAVING A *terrible* BAD-HAIR DAY!"

WHAT'S THE COMPLAINT THAT MEDUSA MAKES?

"I CAN'T DO A THING

WITH THIS HEAD

FULL OF SNAKES!"

CYCLOPS

I've been in sunny Sicily

where the cranky Cyclops roam

with one huge eye in their huge heads

and dreadful mouths that foam.

They rip green olives off the trees,

then store pits in one cheek,

accumulating quite a pile

to spit out when they speak.

So if you go to Sicily

and have the rotten luck

to meet a cranky Cyclops,

be prepared to duck.

Ghost Notes

My files are packed with notes on ghosts,
so I've plucked out just a few
from the folder marked "MUSICIANS."
I hope they'll hum to you:

Franz Schubert (1797—1828)

THE GHOST OF FRANZ SCHUBERT
HAS ALWAYS BEEN PLAGUED
BY A SYMPHONY HE LEFT UNFINISHED.
NOW I LOCK MY PIANO WHEN I GO TO BED,
OR I FIND THAT MY SLEEP IS DIMINISHED.

Louis Armstrong (Satchmo) (1901?—1971)

FIRST A DISTANT TUNE IN BRASS.
NEXT A RASPY VOICE I KNOW...
THEN ALL THE SAINTS COME MARCHING IN
BEHIND
   THE GHOST
      OF OL'...
         SATCHMO!

Elvis Presley (1935—1977)

ELVIS PRESLEY'S FAMED GHOST
WEARS A SHIMMERING SHEET
COVERED WITH SEQUINS AND GLITTER.
THE SHEET SEEMS TOO TIGHT
TO ALLOW FOR FREE FLIGHT,
STILL THE SPECTER CAN BUMP, GRIND, AND FLITTER.

My Favorite Things

Greasy green lizards
and raw chicken gizzards,
spell-binding spells
cast by spell-casting wizards.
Dead mice and head lice
and flapping bat wings—
these are a few of my favorite things!

Bare bones and tombstones
in old cemeteries,
unsweetened pies filled
with wild sour cherries.
Cat claws and rat paws
and bumblebee stings—
these are a few of my favorite things!

Haunting, taunting—
life gets daunting.
That's when this witch sighs,
I simply remember
my favorite things
and fly through October *skies!*

PING-PONG WITH KING KONG

When King Kong plays Ping-Pong,
he squashes the ball.

He whacks it so hard
you can't hit it at all.

But if by some chance
you just happen to score,

he tears down the net
and won't play anymore!

GAME	KONG	M, OLOGIST
1	21	∅
2	21	∅
3	21	∅
4	21	∅
5	21	∅
6	21	∅
7	21	∅
8	21	∅
9	21	∅
	21	∅
	21	∅
12	21	∅
13	21	∅

Chilling Godzilla

RADIOACTIVE FROM HEAD TO TOE,
GODZILLA HAS FINS THAT PULSE AND GLOW.
SINCE HIS ATOMIC BREATH CAN KILL
I NEEDED SOME SORT OF A **POTION** OR **PILL**.
THANKS TO HELP FROM AN ALCHEMIST,
GODZILLA NOW SEEMS TOTALLY BLISSED.
FLAVORED MILK SHAKES **CALM** GODZILLA.
HE SPITS OUT CHOCOLATE BUT LOVES ...**VANILLA!**

怪獣
LAZY LIZARD
Chill Pills
®
ゴジラ

—Fra... ...stein

Car...

Each year or so I see this ad
and feel a helpless chill.
Will some young damsel answer it?
Alas, I know one will.

MEET A MATE

Widower seeks maiden fair
to share a life of ease:
large yachts and gorgeous castle;
right girl gets ALL the keys!
Respond to the address below;
send recent picture, please.

—Bluebeard

General Delivery, London

SEE... ...HERO

...dess...

...dier,

...anyone really,

...olid...R.

...Tell...e all about yo...

...journe...and let...

In a town where I'd not been before
my brow was hot. My throat was sore.
I saw a sign and knocked on the door.

DOCTOR
FRANKENSTEIN

ADVICE FROM

Frankenstein's Monster

You've come to a doctor
I would NEVER recommend.
(Although you're a stranger,
I'm speaking as a friend!)
Doc operates alone by night
in his big laboratory,
and that's where he assembled me,
expecting fame and glory.
He put left feet on two right legs—
used arms that were not matched.
He found a head and body,
but see how they're attached?

Though I'd like to have a buddy,
I began to realize why,
when I saw my own reflection,
I can only…terrify.

AN INTERVIEW WITH THE

Loch Ness

Monster

Tourists flock to Inverness
to glimpse the monster of Loch Ness.
With cameras weighing down their necks,
each and every one expects
to record Nessie doing tricks
with a bunch of click-click-clicks!
Little do they dream that I
am oh so very camera shy
and left the loch some years ago
for places they don't seem to know.

At first I mingled timidly,
amid surrounding scenery.
Loch visitors fulfilled my hope.
They looked at me and saw…a slope.
Then growing bolder, I soon tried
amusement parks where I could ride
the roller coaster undetected—
unpursued and unexpected!
Since then I've traveled far and wide
and find there is no need to hide.
I'll join the opera as a prop.
If I get bored I simply stop.
Attention's easy to escape,
since I know how to drape my shape.
Without an effort at disguise,
I'm unobserved by prying eyes.

I'm careful to suppress the whim
I sometimes get to dive and swim.
In season I observe the shop
where Loch Ness tourists always stop.
But the only swimming I do here,
is up and down a souvenir!

HELICOCRANCHIA PFEFFERI

SOLMISSUS

First seen in 1555...
Norwegians feared they'd not survive!
They thought the Kraken wished to eat
their fleet and crewmen for a treat.

MELANOCETUS JOHNSONI

THE KRAKEN

SCRIPPSIA PACIFICA

AS OUR SUBMARINE DESCENDED,
IT WAS SHAKEN BY A TUG.
THE KRAKEN'S COILING TENTACLES
CLUTCHED IT SNUGLY IN A HUG.
THAT'S THE KRAKEN'S WAY OF SAYING,
"WELCOME! WELCOME! I'M SO PLEASED."
BUT MY CREW GREW VERY NERVOUS
AS THE KRAKEN SQUEEZED AND SQUEEZED.

THE KRAKEN MUST BE LONELY
IN THE DARK DEPTHS OF THE SEA
BUT ITS GREETING UPON MEETING
MUST DISCOURAGE COMPANY!

YETI

Spaghetti

cooking time
11 min.

Enriched Macaroni Product

The Yeti

In the snowy Himalayas
with my trusty Sherpa guide,
I tried to sight a yeti
along the mountainside.
We cooked pots of spaghetti,
which yeti like, I'm told,
covered with tomato sauce,
either hot or cold.
One morning there were footprints
—size twenty-five—
but we never found a yeti
(just some strands of stiff spaghetti).
Yet I'll bet my sister Betty,
that somewhere a hairy yeti
is alive . . .
is *alive.*
Somewhere a hairy yeti is alive.

THE COMPU-MONSTER

HAVE YOU HEARD OF THE COMPU-MONSTER YET?
IT'S CRUISING AROUND THE INTERNET,

INVISIBLY RACING FROM PLACE TO PLACE,

CAUSING CHAOS IN CYBERSPACE.
IT SLIPS AROUND AND MULTIPLIES,

THEN **C R A S H !**

ONE MORE COMPUTER DIES.
AND NOBODY KNOWS

WHEN THIS MONSTER MIGHT
EAT UP THEIR SYSTEM

BYTE

BY

BYTE.

The Verbivore

Librarians should be aware of this menace (although rare).

THINK

DIGS

CALL

USE

VORACIOUSLY, THE VERBIVORE
DINES ON VERBS AND NOTHING MORE.
WHEREVER BOOKS ARE ON A SHELF,
IT SAUNTERS BY AND HELPS ITSELF.
SEEKING ITS SOURCE OF SATISFACTION,
IT STARTS A STORY
AND EATS...
THE ACTION.

PLAY

THROWS

LEAK

GOES

CRAVE

ARE

MIGHT

BEGINS

DIE

THE WORMS ___ IN

Did you ever ___ when a hearse ___ by

That you ___ ___ the next to ___?

An undertaker tall and thin

___ a hole and ___ you in.

All ___ well for about a week,

And then the coffin ___ to ___.

The worms ___ in. The worms ___ out.

The worms ___ pinochle on your snout.

They ___ your bones for telephones

And ___ you up when you ___n't home!

THE SUDS-SURFING SOCK-EATER: A CONJECTURE

Scientific discipline insists I should stay leery
and not assume the truth is found,
when what in truth is theory.
Although I've often seen results,
I have not seen the cause.
Does a monster manage this strange work
with long fangs or sharp claws?

Steeped like a tea bag in mystery,
　　repeatedly eluding me,
　　　　this monster is one I've yet to see.
Yet I know it exists;
Who would dare disagree?
Through the years it persists
　　tantalizingly free
to reduce unto one
that which started as two,
as only a Surfing Sock-Eater would do!

For who does not own a single sock
that once was a part of a pair?
And who can observe a washing machine
without wondering: What's lurking there?
My theory? It's a self-divider:
the Surfing Sock-Eating Bubble-Rider.
Amoeba-shaped to liquidate
any sort of sock it ate
and busy, busy multiplying...
That's the theory I'm implying.

I've lingered in many Laundromats
to watch the soap suds bubble,
I've seen the lonely widowed socks
but not the true cause of their trouble.

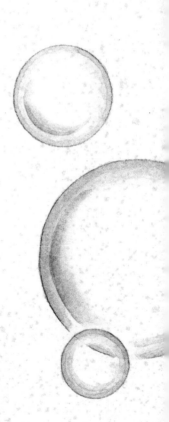

My colleague Will Nixon,
the zombie specialist,
made me an e-mail offer
too tempting to resist.

INTERNATIONAL ZOMBIE SURVEY

Insert ▾   Categories ▾   Projects ▾

From: wnix@mnstru.edu
To: mnstrgist@science.org
Cc:
Subject: INTERNATIONAL ZOMBIE SURVEY
Attachments: none

Courier   11

Funding for my project
has finally come through!
I'm delighted! I'm excited!
There is such good work to do.
Yes, the Undertakers Union
and the Rest in Peace Foundation
will underwrite this research
coast to coast in every nation.
We will take a zombie census,
which has not been done before,
We will profile ALL the living dead
and assign each soul a score!

We've met in Paris and Madrid
at professional conventions.
I've heard your brilliant papers.
You're the thinker thinkers mention.
So when the money was in place,
I closed my eyes and saw...your face!
Would you be my co-director?
Who better than you could I find
for a project so wide-reaching
that demands your kind of mind?

Hoping you agree,
Will Nixon, PhD
****
Monster University, Dept. of the Living Dead

R.I.P.

DR. WM. NIXON, PhD
MONSTER UNIVERSITY
DEPARTMENT OF THE LIVING DEAD

J. K. Carpaton
1266 Rottinga Way
Chicago, Illinois 60606

INTERNATIONAL ZOMBIE SURVEY

As soon as form is completed, subjects will be assigned a number and a country code to protect their privacy and that of their families.

NAME (while a living being)_____

BORN_____ PLACE OF BIRTH_____

DIED_____ PLACE OF DEATH_____

CAUSE OF DEATH (Please circle all that apply)

Zombie bite

Snake or spider bite

Accident (fall, car crash, train wreck, explosion)

Natural causes (decay, old age, fatigue, homework)

Foul play (murder *other than zombie bite*)

Other_____

YOU IN FORMER LIFE (Please circle all that apply)

Male   Female   Short   Tall   Fat   Thin   Just Right

Teacher's Pet   Class Clown   Hall Monitor

Tattle Tale   Life of the Party   Shy   Kind   Bully

Always Hungry

Other_____

EATING HABITS

☐ Member of Clean Plate Club

☐ Food Fussy

☐ Vegetarian

☐ Vegetarian (with Fish & Chicken)

☐ Vegan

HOW MANY ZOMBIES HAVE YOU ADDED TO THE PACK SINCE YOU BECAME ONE YOURSELF?

☐ 0-5   ☐ 6-20   ☐ 21-49   ☐ 100 or more   ☐ no idea

WHAT IS YOUR FAVORITE BODY PART?_____

DO YOU CONSIDER YOURSELF AN EQUAL-OPPORTUNITY EATER?

☐ yes   ☐ no

Thank you for participating in this survey.

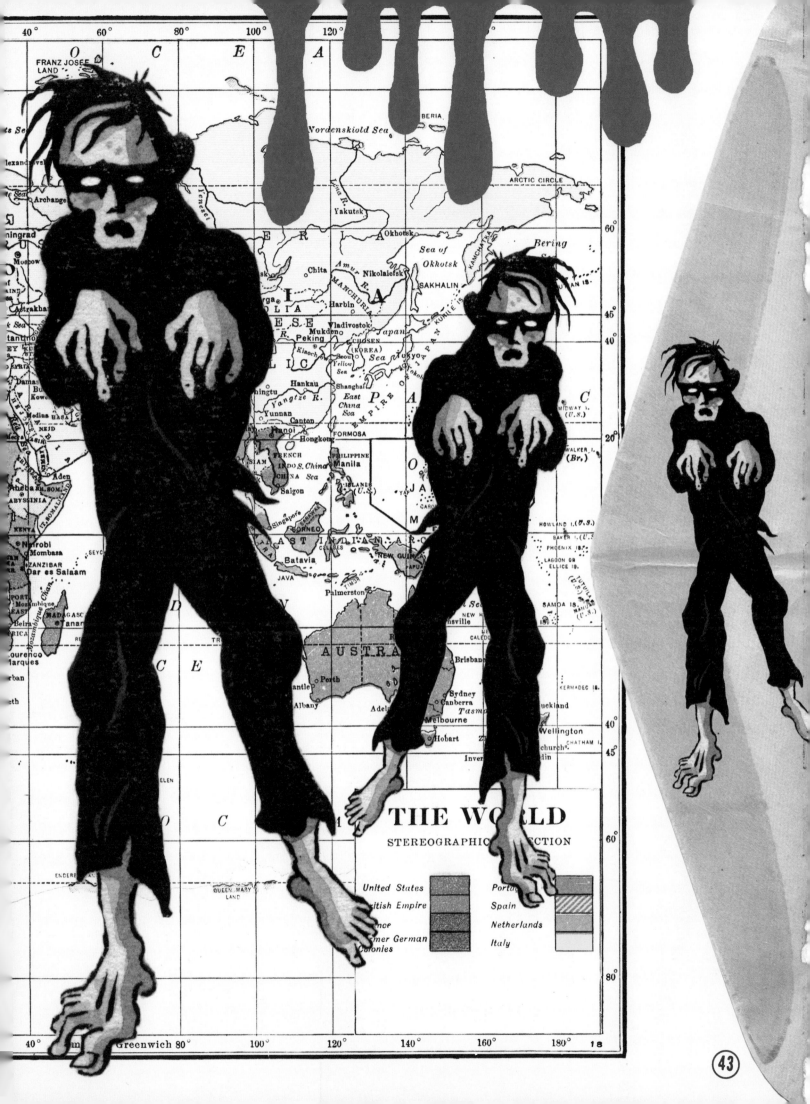

A Suggestion for My Readers

Years ago when I was young,
I found it hard to say
what I would be when I grew up
and had a job someday.
Perhaps if people ask you
what you are going to be,
you'll choose a fine career like mine—

in Monsterology!

ACKNOWLEDGMENTS TO MY RESEARCH ASSISTANTS

Bobbi Katz Ghostwriter Extraordinaire

Bobbi Katz was playing ping-pong with King Kong when we met twenty years ago. She told me about her many books and I told her about my work with monsters. When her book Once Around the Sun was on a list of the year's ten best poetry books, I gave her flowers. (A funeral had taken place just hours earlier and they were still very fresh!)

When a New York Times book reviewer wrote, "Bobbi Katz does everything right," all was clear. She's written biographies, novels, picture books, and piles of poems. Why not a memoir... in rhyme? And who knows me better? I believe The Monsterologist is her 13th collection of poems. Manhattan and upstate New York are her favorite haunts. You may visit Bobbi at www.bobbikatz.com.

Adam McCauley Supernatural Image Specialist

Adam McCauley of San Francisco came highly recommended by Dr. Nixon, the zombie specialist, who found it endearing that Adam was once terrified of Hollywood monsters, but grew to love the Tales from the Crypt comics. As you can see, Adam has developed into quite a monster specialist himself.

Adam's work has been included in group shows in New York, Nashville, Los Angeles, Osaka, and Tokyo, where I met him while researching Godzilla. Adam has illustrated numerous books for young readers, including Jon Scieszka's popular Time Warp Trio series and Richard Michelson's Oh No, Not Ghosts! He was awarded a gold medal by the Society of Illustrators for the art featured on the endpapers of my handsome memoir. You may visit Adam online at www.adammccauley.com.

A RARE CHANCE MEETING WITH A REPRESENTATIVE FROM ZARGON 9

SCENIC
TRANSYLVANIA
"TRANSPORT YOURSELF"

EVER
ON
Greyhound Lines